FLAMESON

by

KATHRYN HAYTER

ARTHUR H. STOCKWELL LTD
Torrs Park   Ilfracombe   Devon
Established 1898
www.ahstockwell.co.uk

© Kathryn Hayter, 2018
First published in Great Britain, 2018

The moral rights of the author have been asserted.

All rights reserved.
No part of this publication may be reproduced
or transmitted in any form or by any means,
electronic or mechanical, including photocopy,
recording, or any information storage and
retrieval system, without permission
in writing from the copyright holder.

British Library Cataloguing-in-Publication Data.
A catalogue record for this book is available
from the British Library.

DEDICATION

To my most precious Mum and Dad.

ISBN 978-0-7223-4907-6
Printed in Great Britain by
Arthur H. Stockwell Ltd
Torrs Park   Ilfracombe
Devon EX34 8BA

CONTENTS

ENCOUNTER   5

Chapter One   ON BIG BEN   14

Chapter Two   IN REGENT'S PARK   34

Chapter Three IN LONDON ZOO   50

Chapter Four   ON PRIMROSE HILL   82

ENCOUNTER

The proud English oak had stood for 100 years. Children laughed and learned beneath it. Once a year they gathered around it, gazing up at it in admiration and solemn reflection. They loved the old oak – it was brave, sturdy, strong and full of history. But they never really spoke about the oak until the day they heard it sing.

The students shuffled into the school hall as usual and sat silently, waiting for assembly to start. The room was crowded; and even though the windows were wide open, it was still stuffy and hot and the mood seemed subdued. Most were lost in their own thoughts, dreaming about somewhere they would rather be.

And then, from the back of the hall, they heard his voice and the room seemed bigger and the air felt fresher. His full-throttled fanfare filled their ears and he sang with an energy and truth that touched their hearts and made their spirits soar. His song seemed angelic, fearless, joyful, a celebration of creation! Every child turned to locate the source of the song and each could feel his steady, bright-eyed gaze before they saw his red heart, flaming from the top of the old oak.

The children were in the company of Rejoice the Robin. Rejoice was perched on the school war memorial, three fine oak panels on the back wall of the hall which contained the names of students and staff who had died in World Wars One and Two. On that normal school day, the proud oak memorial had come to life in the magnificent song of Rejoice the Robin. From then on, they often spoke about the old oak and the day they heard it sing.

When did you last see a robin? Was he high in a tree or hidden in a hedge? Or perhaps he flew on to a fork handle in the garden? Robins turn up all over the place and perch on all sorts of things. From flowerpots to flagpoles and teapots to traffic lights, the redbreast can be found sitting on almost anything that takes his fancy, affirms his territory and feeds his curiosity – and his appetite!

Like many other birds, Rejoice the Robin can be spotted up in treetops asserting his identity, and down on the ground

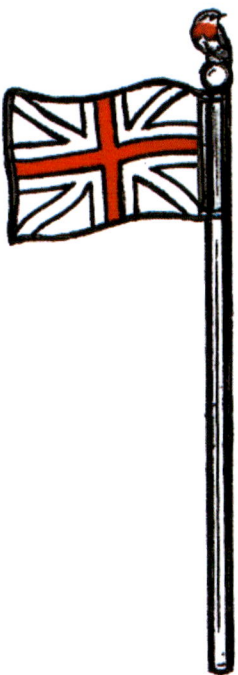

foraging for fragments of food. But it can't really be said that Rejoice is like most other birds. In fact, Rejoice isn't like any other bird because, although he appears in all the usual robin places and does the usual robin things, he also turns up in unusual places and does unusual things. He is, indeed, a most unusual robin – a bird blessed with a special song to sing.

Rejoice is a musical messenger, a joyful singing heart. On wise wings he brings glad tidings and tells tuneful, timeless tales full of ancient truths. He comes from a long line of rare robins who, in a relay of song, pass on a rich inheritance of history-hymns and memory treasures from century to century to enlighten the world they live in.

And how he loves history! Rejoice travels far and wide to find it. He flies much further than other robins and is not restricted by distance or territory. Like his ancestors before him, Rejoice soars across the land looking for history to sit on and sing about. He searches for statues and sculptures, memorials and monuments, art and architecture to perch and ponder on. He hunts for the heroes of history who have something to say to help us today, and he celebrates them. . . . Rejoice loves to celebrate!

Throughout the year, on their birthdays and anniversaries, the robin gives his gift of song to celebrate and honour them. But he gives his best song gift when he celebrates the most

important birthday of the year – on Christmas Day.

On Christmas Day the robin sings with greater strength than on any other day of the year because Christmas Day is his favourite anniversary. It is a day when time stands still, a day when all creation, past, present and future, is invited to come close to a cradle and celebrate the birthday of Love. And Rejoice always accepts His invitation!

On Christmas Eve Rejoice prepares to celebrate. He gets ready to deliver his birthday song gift, the Christmas Day carol, a Flamesong lit by the love in his heart. As the clocks chime at midnight on Christmas Eve, Rejoice jingles with joy and rings out his carol. But how will he choose his Christmas hymn? Which carol will the bellbird ring? What message will the robin bring? Which Flamesong will he find to sing?

Watch and wait for robin wings,
Listen and hear the redbreast sing!
Places to go, people to see,
His name is Rejoice, he sings history.
High on a branch up in a tree,
He sings of the year's anniversaries.
Tune tales will be told about heroes of old
Who have something to say to help us today.
An old year must end with a message to send,
A deep truth to be found as the Christmas bells sound.
The robin will bring a Flamesong to sing
And his carol will rhyme at the twelve-o'clock chime.

Rejoice! Rejoice! Sing out in joyful voice!
And let us hear, with heart and ear,
The tune tales of your choice. . . .

Chapter One

ON BIG BEN

It was dawn on Christmas Eve and Rejoice the Robin only had fifteen minutes to welcome the new day in song before his tiny feathered body would be blown off the belfry in the force of the giant bell's vibrations.

Every year on 24 December, Rejoice wings his way into central London to visit the nation's heartbeat, Big Ben. He sits on a ledge in the belfry above the big clock's famous four faces and, between the Westminster chimes of the quarterly bells which ring out the music of Handel's *Messiah*, Rejoice proclaims his own credo. He sings a song of belief, a song of waiting and anticipation, a song of expectation and excitement, a song which tells the world to get ready to celebrate Christmas:

> Ding dong merrily on high,
> In Heaven the bells are ringing,
> Ding dong verily the sky
> Is riven with angels singing.
> Gloria, in Excelsis Deo!
> Gloria, in Excelsis Deo!

On Christmas Eve, Rejoice prepares to celebrate the best birthday of the year, the greatest birthday of all time. But the robin loves to look for anniversaries on every other day of the year too. Throughout the year, he makes it his mission to search for the heroes of history and celebrate their anniversaries in song. During the last twelve months he had sat on and sung about several heroes and, in the cold December dawn, even though the winter sun had not yet risen very high in the sky, the robin could spot some of them from the belfry.

Rejoice looked down at Parliament Square beneath Big Ben, where the figures of several heroes stand, and still speak to people's hearts. He often visited them, fluttering around their faces then sitting on their statues and singing their songs to the passing world. Rejoice would chirp cheerfully at Churchill as he sat on his shoulder and sang his encouraging message:

Never, never give up; never, never give up.

And then the little bird would fly across the square to land on Gandhi's glasses and gaze into his wise eyes. These eyes had seen a peaceful way to live. The gentle Indian had called people to turn away from violence and treat each other with respect, and Rejoice was always happy to sing his positive song:

Be the change you want to see,
Follow the Truth who will set you free,
An eye for an eye and the world will be blind,
Find a way to forgive, find a way to be kind.

If he hopped up on to Gandhi's smooth polished head and turned his tiny body to the right, Rejoice could look towards Westminster Abbey, towering over the square in spiritual splendour. This year, back in April, the robin had made a special visit to its great West Door, where the figure of Dr Martin Luther King stands in stone with nine other Christian martyrs. Rejoice had sat on the abbey railings beneath his hero to sing him an anniversary song, and he was sure that the beautiful black Baptist preacher had heard it:

> Great orator, your dream delights,
> Your words inspire and shine a light
> On prejudice and pain and plight,
> On souls deprived of equal rights.
> Great prophet man, your passion speech
> Still stirs the heart and moves the feet
> Of freedom folk who flee from fear,
> And even now they turn to hear
> Your call for justice ringing clear
> From mountaintop to ocean floor,
> And just as powerful as before
> Your mighty message tears through time,
> Your dream delights our hearts and minds.
> Dear Dr King, great preacher man,
> You took us gently by the hand
> And taught us how to understand
> That Love will find the Promised Land.

From his belfry ledge, the small robin looked out to locate the statue of another great leader down in Parliament Square. Nelson Mandela was still standing solid and strong and sure with arms outstretched, inviting people to listen and learn. Rejoice loved perching on his hand to celebrate the hero in song, and this year there was much to sing

about because it had been Nelson's 100th birthday.

Mandela never gave up. Born in 1918, his fight against racism in South Africa led to twenty-seven years of imprisonment. Nelson survived his captivity and went on to create a Rainbow Nation in which many people of different colour and race live and work peacefully together.

Rejoice liked this idea a lot, for in his heart he knew that every creature on earth is born to be different, but each is equally valued by its Creator.

'How dull life would be if every bird sang the same song,' thought the robin up on his lofty ledge, as he surveyed the statues standing in the square.

Like the big cracked bell hanging behind him, the heroes were not without their flaws and faults, but, in very different voices, they had all called people to stand up to injustice with courage and determination, and the whole world had listened. Nelson Mandela's brave call still echoed across the years like thunder in the mountains, inspiring millions to begin their own long walk to freedom; and whenever Rejoice flew into the square to visit Nelson, the robin would alight with delight on a favourite perch – the forefinger of the hero's left hand – where he would sing Nelson's song at the top of his voice:

> Come gather near with ears to hear,
> Courage will triumph over fear!

Mandela had commanded great respect. He even had a species of spider named after him.

'That's one spider I would never eat,' mused the robin, and slightly alarmed by the passing thought of eating Nelson, he flew to another corner of the belfry.

From his new position, Rejoice had a wonderful window on Westminster, and in the pale Yule-light he looked towards Victoria Tower Gardens, where Emmeline Pankhurst stands in the shadow of Parliament. He had perched on her statue in the summer to sing about the 160th anniversary of her birth. Now, as he sat in the cool pre-chime calm of the belfry, Rejoice thought about the suffragette and the turbulent times she had lived through.

The tiny robin looked down at the tall black railings beneath Big Ben which enclose and protect Parliament. He had heard that women once chained themselves to railings like these. The black iron fence that fortifies Parliament had once kept women out of government and had become a platform of protest and publicity for Emmeline and her suffragettes, who came to Westminster to campaign for equal rights. One hundred years ago, they had lived in a man's world in which many women were given little respect and were treated cruelly and unfairly. Without a

vote, a political voice, they were powerless to improve their lives. Emmeline, her daughters and her sisters, had fought hard to give women a voice, enduring torture and imprisonment in their struggle to be heard. And their voice was eventually heard. In 1918, having made an important contribution during World War One, many women won the right to have a say in British government for the very first time.

Some, like suffragist Millicent Fawcett, the only female bronze figure in Parliament Square, said that Emmeline was too forceful in her fight for justice and equality. But Rejoice, being a robin, admired Emmeline's fearless determination. Her statue was small, but, like the tiny bird, she had sung a strong, spirited and significant song and Rejoice was always excited to sit on the suffragette and sing about her sacrifice and service:

Great was the challenge and long was the struggle,
But Emmeline battled through turmoil and trouble.
Her clear call for action was heeded and heard –
Join the journey for justice, deeds speak louder than words!

'Emmeline never gave up,' thought the robin, his red breast blazing from the belfry like a beacon.

She suffered and struggled for her cause, but like a butterfly emerging from its cocoon, the brave suffragette and her suffragist sisters had pushed through difficulty to fly towards freedom on strong purple, white and green wings.

It would soon be time for the robin's wings to fly from the belfry, for the quarterly chime would strike in a short while and, at the thought of bells, Rejoice turned on his ledge to look at the most famous bell in the world, Big Ben. Now hanging silent and still, this faithful bell was sure to sing his familiar song, on the hour, every hour. Ben is big, very big. As heavy as a small elephant, he hangs in the belfry three hundred and thirty-four steps above ground level, and, like the robin, he rings with the rhythms of history and sings the tunes of time. Perching high on Big Ben reminded Rejoice of sitting up in a very tall tree, and from his belfry branch the robin had a wonderful view of the London skyline.

On this Christmas Eve morning, a winter sun slowly rose over the great city and Rejoice's spirits rose too. The robin's heart glowed as he gazed out at a frosty urban forest of flagged towers and turrets, rooftops and chimneys, spires and skyscrapers. The frozen city forest was now beginning

to thaw in the strengthening sunlight, and Rejoice fluffed out his feathers in delight at the realisation of being alive on such a morning in such a place. The Shard shimmered in the distance. Wembley's white arch shone too in the dazzling dawn and the London Eye winked and twinkled as it prepared for its first flight of the day. London was waking up. Trains, traffic and tourists were already on the move – a tuneful travelling choir, turning up the volume in an urban dawn chorus.

Suddenly, Rejoice felt a sense of purpose and urgency. He had a busy day ahead of him, for Christmas Eve is always a time of preparation. Today Rejoice had an important job to do because today he had to choose his carol – the Christmas Day carol. Tonight the robin would return to Big Ben and, as soon as the great bell had rung out its midnight chime, Rejoice would ring out his Christmas hymn.

The choice would not be easy since there were so many beautiful carols to choose from, but Rejoice knew he would enjoy making his decision and he looked forward to finding his Flamesong. The robin would spend Christmas Eve in reflection. He would continue to think about the anniversaries he had celebrated during the year and he would look for more inspiration from all the history and the heroes he had sat on and sung about. By the end of the day he would have

chosen his musical message, and tomorrow he would sing a carol the world needed to hear.

A breeze began to blow through the belfry, ruffling the robin's feathers. It was time to leave Big Ben. The quarterly chime would begin in a few minutes and Rejoice had to be gone before the bells sounded.

The robin looked out across London. Where could he continue his reflections? Rejoice turned his head towards the north and scanned the skyline. His gaze fell in the direction of Primrose Hill, in Regent's Park.

'Will I find my Christmas Day carol there?'

Rejoice couldn't answer his own question, but he knew that this was where he must fly first. And as he flew towards the north, a melody echoed in the robin's ears:

> Hills of the north, rejoice!
> Songs be on every wing.
> Hark to the advent voice!
> River and city, sing!
> Let angels' anthems fill the earth,
> All hearts await the Saviour's birth!

Chapter Two

IN REGENT'S PARK

London has eight royal parks. Rejoice the Robin loves visiting all of them, but Regent's Park, the jewel in the crown, is probably his favourite.

As he flew into north-west London on this crisp Christmas Eve morning, Rejoice enjoyed a bird's-eye view of the green jewel glistening beneath him. Winter sunbeams danced on the surface of the park's large lake and glossed the grassy, rounded summit of Primrose Hill, which rose up gently on the park's northern side.

The robin began his descent and touched down in Queen Mary's Gardens, landing lightly on the top of a boy's head – not a human head, but a head made of bronze, which belonged to a boy who sat in a pond holding a frog. The figure stood in a formal space near the rose garden. Rejoice

perched on the boy in a pert, purposeful pose, and while the boy gazed contentedly at the creature in his hand the robin peered down at the pond water, contemplating the task that lay before him. He didn't have much time to choose the carol he would sing tomorrow on Christmas Day, so the redbreast settled himself to continue his reflections. He thought deeply.

'Which carol do human hearts need to heed this year?'

Rejoice hoped he would find an answer to his question from the people he had seen and the places he had been during the past twelve months. Where had he spent his time? There had certainly been much to celebrate in central London; being a bird, the robin liked to spend a lot of his time in green spaces, and where better than the green jewel? The park was indeed full of jewels and gems, and Rejoice sat up straight on the boy's head, his bright eyes shining, as he pictured the thousands and thousands of roses around him. Each plant was now neatly pruned and empty of perfume, but the robin could remember the rose garden in summer when the bushes were vibrant with colour and the air was heavy with scent. And as he thought about Queen Mary's royal roses, Rejoice began to

reminisce about the many happy hours he had enjoyed in Regent's Park. He knew and loved every colourful corner of it.

Sometimes he would fly over to The Hub, where the robin would sit on goalposts to cheer footballers and rugby players perfecting their game. Despite being an independent bird who was very happy in his own company, Rejoice liked to watch team sports, and he was always eager to encourage and support, hopping around the sidelines of a muddy pitch during matches and balancing on any stray ball that came his way.

Sometimes he would pop into the park's open-air theatre to watch its productions, and now and again, when he felt like it, he would fly on to the stage and perch on part of the set so that he could sing his songs to the public, who always seemed to appreciate his performance since they clapped very loudly. But he spent most of his time over in the Allotment Garden, where he could frequently be found bobbing about in freshly dug soil and filling his stomach with worms.

Rejoice was not the only bird who benefitted from the rich resources on offer in Regent's Park. The oldest inhabitants in the green jewel were its trees – the lungs of London. Birds of every shape, colour and size sat, slept and sang in them – tawny owls, green woodpeckers, kestrels and blackbirds, to name but a few, could be spotted in the park's old English oaks. And Rejoice was not the only robin to spend time in Regent's Park, although he certainly was the most unusual! The jewel was large enough to offer a home to many territorial robins.

Rejoice knew that, during the breeding season, some of them made their nests in tree-trunk holes, while others chose to build in more unusual locations. Rejoice, being Rejoice, always encouraged his mate to construct her nest in the most obscure place possible. One year she decided to build it in a large lost woolly glove that had found its way into a hedge and hung like a hammock as a cosy cradle for her five Tiffany-blue eggs. The old glove had provided a useful source of hair and wool with which to weave and line the leafy, mossy nest, and Rejoice had been most grateful to the glove for lending a helping hand!

The park certainly had a lot to offer, and the robin never tired of reminiscing about the happy hours he had spent in it and the many memories he had made in it, but now the little bird was hungry and his attention turned to food. Since he wanted something sweet to eat, Rejoice decided to leave the boy and the frog, and wing his way over to the Boathouse Café on the lake, where he was sure to find some tasty treats on the terrace. So off he flew, and in no time at all Rejoice was hopping around under the tables searching for crumbs – especially fruit-cake crumbs, to which he was particularly partial.

After pecking about for a while, and dodging a determined grey squirrel who delighted in jumping in and out of rubbish bins, Rejoice flew up on to the roof of the café to return to his thoughts. From here he had a good view of the lake and its swans, and he sat quietly, looking at winter reflections in the water and waiting for inspiration.

Time was passing by. Rejoice hadn't yet thought of the Christmas Day carol he would deliver tomorrow. But, as he gazed at the boating lake, his musings were interrupted by a melody and he felt inclined to sing:

I saw three ships come sailing in,
On Christmas Day, on Christmas Day,
I saw three ships come sailing in,
On Christmas Day in the morning!

And what was in those ships all three,
On Christmas Day, on Christmas Day,
And what was in those ships all three,
On Christmas Day in the morning?

Our Saviour Christ and His Lady,
On Christmas Day, on Christmas Day,
Our Saviour Christ and His Lady,
On Christmas Day in the morning!

And all the bells on earth shall ring,
On Christmas Day, on Christmas Day,
And all the angels in Heaven shall sing,
On Christmas Day in the morning!

> Then let us all rejoice amen,
> On Christmas Day, on Christmas Day,
> Then let us all rejoice amen,
> On Christmas Day in the morning!

The robin finished singing his merry melody and, feeling very festive, he asked himself a question: 'Could this be my Christmas Day carol?'

He wasn't sure. It was a song of joy and good news that a troubled world needed to hear and it was certainly a song of celebration. Rejoice could never resist an opportunity to celebrate, especially on Christmas Day, since there was so much love to be thankful for. The little bird felt that he might have found what he was looking for, but he wanted to sing a few more carols and think a few more thoughts before he made his final choice. In any case, his song had certainly put him in the mood for fun, and fortunately he knew he wouldn't have to look far to find it! Rejoice was familiar with a place in the park that was full of fun. In fact, it was full of fun and feathers and fur and fish and food (which was always on

his mind) and so, with the festive carol still ringing in his ears, he left the Boathouse Café and flew off towards the northern edge of Regent's Park. His destination was London Zoo.

Chapter Three

IN LONDON ZOO

Rejoice could hear the zoo before he saw it. Sounds of excited chatter from the monkeys signalled to the robin that he was fast approaching an exotic corner of London, where a noisy Noah's Ark was home to thousands of creatures – lions, tigers, gorillas, zebras, giraffes, hippos, kangaroos and, of course, the ever popular penguins.

As he flew towards the zoo in the cool winter air, Rejoice felt freedom filtering through his feathers and a sense of wide, open space all around him. He thought of the enclosed creatures on the ground below and he wished that they could escape their captivity and return to the wild. But the robin reminded himself that life was not always straightforward. Many of the animals belonged to endangered species and the zoo did good work in

conservation. It certainly took care of its scaly and hairy inhabitants, who usually seemed happy whenever Rejoice visited them.

The robin navigated his way to the Blackburn Pavilion clock outside the entrance to the Tropical Bird House. Rejoice liked clocks and made a habit of sitting on them. In fact, whenever he saw a clock he would sit on it – unless it was a cuckoo clock, of course, which he tended to avoid. The robin often perched on the top of the pavilion clock and always made sure that he arrived in time to watch its display. Every thirty minutes, eight disappearing birds would reappear, one by one, around the edges of the clock face. Rejoice quivered with delight as he sat on the large, comical timepiece, waiting for the display to start, and as he waited he thought of all the anniversaries he had celebrated in the zoo during the past twelve months. There had been much to sing about. London Zoo had enjoyed its own 190th birthday this year. First opened in 1828, it was the world's oldest scientific zoo, and Rejoice, along with thousands of other visitors, spent a lot of time in it, not least because it offered him an endless source of food!

The Blackburn birds finished their display and the robin glanced down at the large clock face beneath him. Time was moving on. Rejoice had to choose his Christmas Day carol as soon as possible, and he needed to find inspiration fast, so he flew off across the zoo to look for a legend.

He went in search of an ape.

It wasn't difficult to spot the gorilla. The little bird landed on the back of the huge animal in a clumsy fashion almost skidding off the creature, not because it was large and intimidating, but because this particular gorilla's back was smooth and polished and, like the boy and the frog, was made of bronze. The ape had arrived at the zoo in 1947 on Guy Fawkes Night.

'It wouldn't be hard to guess this creature's name!' thought Rejoice as he settled himself on the statue and gazed at Guy with great affection.

The gorilla had arrived at the zoo as a tiny baby, holding a small tin hot-water bottle, and had grown into a massive ape with a fearsome appearance. Yet he was a gentle giant. Strong but sensitive, tough but tender, he was loved by

many. Rejoice cherished a beautiful memory treasure that had been passed down, robin to robin, from his great-great-great-great-great-grandfather, who had once flown into Guy's cage. The gorilla had lifted the tiny robin in his large hands and had spent some time looking lovingly at the small bird before carefully letting him go.

'What an awesome animal!' mused Rejoice, his eyes twinkling as he considered the curious connections and wonderful relationships which exist between all living things.

And Guy was not the only famous ape to have lived in the zoo. There was Jenny – the orangutan. When a certain Charles Darwin saw Jenny studying herself in a mirror one hundred and eighty years ago, he looked at himself more closely and reflected on his relationship with the ape. His observations became part of a theory that introduced the world to the idea of evolution.

The robin bobbed along Guy's big bronze back and hopped up on to the gorilla's head, cheeping and chatting to people passing by:

> Footprints to follow, tune tracks to find,
> Sing of the heroes trailblazing through time.

And then, with his thoughts full of hairy history, he left Guy to search for more inspiration, this time in the shape of a bear – a bear named Winnie. The zoo was buzzing below the red-breasted bird in Christmas Eve excitement as he flew off to look for the bear. As usual, Rejoice headed in the direction of a café, and immediately located Winnie. He dropped down decisively on to her upturned nose and sat between her eyes.

From his vantage point, the robin had a clear view of a soldier dressed in full military uniform who stood in front of the bear, holding her paw in his hand. But neither the animal nor the soldier moved a muscle because Rejoice was perched on a sculpture – a statue of a soldier who had fought in World War One and an American black bear.

Theirs was a story of love and loyalty, a memory treasure that had been passed down to Rejoice from his ancestors; and although the robin had been told their tale many times,

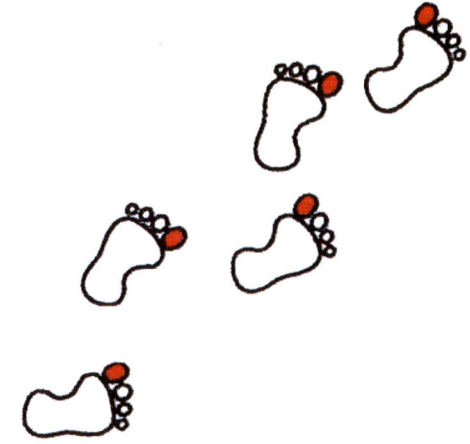

he had never tired of hearing it. And so, on this sunny Christmas Eve, he fluffed his feathers and puffed out his body into a ball as he nestled on Winnie's nose and began to reflect on their beautiful relationship.

On 24 August 1914, veterinary officer Lieutenant Harry Colebourn was travelling from Canada to Europe to fight in the First World War. During the journey, Harry had a train stop at White River, Ontario, where he bought a black bear cub for $20 from a hunter who had killed the bear's mother. Colebourn called the bear Winnie after Winnipeg, his Canadian home town, and took her to Wiltshire in England where his regiment was training on Salisbury Plain. The bear became the soldiers' pet and the mascot of their regiment. With a thick, glossy black coat and a tan muzzle, she brought joy to the soldiers, following them around the camp like a dog, climbing up and down tent poles and playing hide and seek with them. Winnie slept under Harry's bed at night and, like Rejoice, always hungry, she enjoyed small bottles of condensed milk during the day. Harry and Winnie developed a deep and devoted affection for each other – so much so that when

Harry had to leave Winnie for three years to fight in France on the Western Front, he found solace in thinking about the beautiful bond he had made with his beloved bear back in England. And Harry had to hold on tight to his happy thoughts because, like thousands of other soldiers, he was joining an horrific war in which millions of people and animals died. And even now, as he sat on Winnie's shiny nose, the robin's tiny body trembled as he recalled the terrible tales his ancestors had told about it.

World War One was a cruel and complicated conflict which dragged on for four years and changed the world forever. Rejoice couldn't make sense of it. He knew all about defending territory, for robins can be very aggressive when challenged by other robins. But although Rejoice could be feisty, he was a rare bird who was not tied down by type or temperament and he knew when it was time to fly above and away from a fight. He certainly couldn't get his feathered head around most human conflicts.

The First World War was fought all over the world. Some of the worst fighting had taken place in Belgium

and France on the Western Front, where men lived in trenches (roofless tunnels) and fought each other with deadly weapons such as poison gas, which blinded and suffocated the soldiers. It was a messy, muddy, monotonous war full of madness and misjudgements in which machine guns and mustard gas maimed and mangled men's minds and bodies and assaulted their senses.

This was the war that Harry Colebourn and so many other soldiers had joined in 1914, and Rejoice still shuddered at the very thought of it. But during his weeks of training on Salisbury Plain, Harry and his regiment had gained comfort in the company of a gentle creature – a bear whom they grew to love – and they took their precious memories of Winnie to the Western Front with them, memories which helped to heal their shattered minds and soothe their splintered spirits.

Before Harry left for France, he put Winnie in London Zoo for safekeeping. When he returned from the war, the soldier was reunited with his old furry friend. On finding her happy and healthy, Harry decided to let Winnie

remain in the zoo, and there she stayed for twenty years, delighting visitors every day with her playful, gentle nature.

The robin hopped to the back of the bear's bronze head and sat close to her left ear, his flaming breast flickering with affection. He whispered softly to Winnie, so softly and quietly that only the bear could hear his musical murmur:

> Dear gentle bear, you did not choose
> To live your life inside a zoo.
> You did not plan to spend your days
> In army camp and public gaze.
> Yet, faithful friend with furry face,
> You made the world a better place;
> And though not wild and free to roam,
> In human hearts you found a home.

Rejoice flew up on to Harry's hat and, tilting his head, the robin looked down at Winnie in fond admiration and deep respect. He knew so many stories about courageous

creatures who, with devotion and loyalty, provided comfort, inspiration and service during World War One. Their sacrifice was great. Over eight million horses, mules and donkeys died during the conflict and many other creatures were badly wounded. Rejoice had heard of a pigeon called Cher Ami who was injured when delivering a message to soldiers in France. Despite losing an eye and a leg, she managed to save nearly two hundred lives, and after the war she was given a hero's welcome home . . . and a wooden leg!

Rejoice had also heard tales about tails – stories of four-legged canine heroes who had seen action in the Great War. Sergeant Stubby, a Staffordshire terrier who could salute with his right paw, served in seventeen battles and received numerous medals for saving many lives. Stubby's sense of smell allowed him to detect enemy gas before the soldiers inhaled and choked on it. When the dog barked to warn them of poison gas, the soldiers put on their masks and protected themselves from its fatal fumes.

Rejoice remembered that his great-great-great-great-great-great-great-great-great-great-grandfather even saw

slugs serving in World War One! Like Stubby, the slugs saved soldiers' lives because they detected mustard gas before humans could smell it. They would show their discomfort by closing their breathing pores and compressing their bodies. This was the slugs' signal for soldiers to put on their gas masks.

'Three cheers for the Slug Brigade,' chirped the robin as he flapped and clapped his wings in appreciation, and he vowed that he would never snack on a slug again.

Rejoice always felt inspired by the stories of birds and animals who had served in World War One, and his memory treasures moved him to make more melody. The robin knew that he must find his Christmas Day carol before the day was over, and so, as he sat on Harry's hat in the happy hubbub of London Zoo, Rejoice began to sing.

His stable song was a tribute to all the creatures in history who have given themselves, in love and loyalty, to the service of others and have been blessed with a special closeness to their Creator because of it:

Away in a manger, no crib for a bed,
The little Lord Jesus lay down His sweet head.
The stars in the bright sky looked down where He lay,
The little Lord Jesus, asleep on the hay.

The cattle are lowing, the Baby awakes,
But little Lord Jesus no crying He makes.
I love Thee, Lord Jesus, look down from the sky,
And stay by my side until morning is nigh.

Be near me, Lord Jesus, I ask Thee to stay
Close by me forever, and love me, I pray.
Bless all the dear children in Thy tender care,
And fit us for Heaven to live with Thee there.

Rejoice finished his carol, feeling full of hope. He had sung three carols already that day and he still had several hours of Christmas Eve left in which to make his carol choice.

'I am sure to find my gift song before nightfall,' thought the robin as he hopped off Harry's hat and dropped to the ground to find more food.

Rejoice was now ravenous. To his delight, he quickly spotted something to eat, and it was sweet! The bird bounced around on the ground, surveying his snack, but he was soon disappointed by his discovery. Several lumps of brightly coloured food lay scattered around him – more than enough to make a tasty meal – but when he took a small peck out of one of them he found himself with a beak full of pink sugary jelly, which he found difficult to swallow and even more difficult to get rid of. Rejoice wiped his beak from side to side on the ground. He didn't like the food at all, but he did recognise it. The robin remembered that he had seen the coloured lumps before, and, although he was slightly annoyed by his sticky bill, he was pleased to have come face-to-face with yet more history. It was all over the place. In fact, it was everywhere he looked! Rejoice was surrounded by smiling Jelly Babies, clearly dropped from a height by a hungry human. First sold in 1918 to celebrate the end of World War One, the sweets were originally called Peace Babies; and now here they were staring at the ravenous redbreast, who continued to scrape off the sugary substance from

his bill with rhythmic determination. Then, with peace on his mind and jelly in his belly, the sticky robin finished wiping his beak and winged his way over to the Three Island Pond to have a bath and a drink.

As its name suggests, the zoo's Three Island Pond is a pond with three islands in it, populated by pelicans and flamingos. Having cleaned and preened himself, Rejoice rested quietly by the edge of the pond, gazing into its cold water. He thought of Harry and Winnie and he pictured the Peace Babies scattered on the ground around them. Maybe he had been looking at pink flamingos for too long, but Rejoice was sure that he could see the jolly jellies smiling at him in the water! The pond was full of reflections, and so was the robin, who began to think deeply about the peace sweets and everything they stood for.

Suddenly, Rejoice looked up from the water and realised where he was. He knew that he was in the presence of something special and, at the same time, something familiar. He turned his tiny body towards the Butterfly

House, the fine feathers on his forehead lifting slightly as if brushed by a light breeze. There, standing alone in Portland stone, he saw Peace.

The robin flew over to it and perched on it. Rejoice had landed on the zoo's war memorial. Designed like a lantern, the memorial was inscribed with the names of staff from London Zoo who served and died in World War One, and the flame on the robin's breast burned brightly as he thought about its significance.

He had been here before, back in November, when at eleven o'clock on the eleventh day of the eleventh month the world had paused for two minutes to remember the Armistice – the ceasefire which ended the First World War one hundred years ago. Rejoice recalled the peace he had heard on that Armistice Sunday, when people placed their poppies on the memorial in remembrance of the Glorious Dead. The robin had worn his own poppy and had sung his own Armistice anniversary song, when at eleven o'clock he had broken the silence in deep-throated thanks for valiant hearts who had lived and died for love:

Remember them when the sun goes down,
When the day is done and the birds have flown,
And when night has passed, during dawn's first flight,
Remember them in the morning light.

The winter sun would soon be going down on the robin's Christmas Eve reflections, and in the morning he would sing to remember the birth of the greatest love of all. But Rejoice had still not chosen his Christmas Day carol. It was time to leave London Zoo and return to the park.

Chapter Four

ON PRIMROSE HILL

Rejoice returned to Regent's Park to find a lot of twittering and tweeting, but it wasn't coming from the birds. The park had seen a lot of visitors that day, and now, as Christmas Eve ebbed away and the light began to fade, some of them were lingering in cafés on laptops while others were still sitting on benches, lost in textland.

"I told you to buy the jumper with the fat snowman on it," said one angry woman into her phone. "Now it's too late and I'll have nothing to wear."

Rejoice listened to the loud lady as he perched beside her on the back of her bench. The robin shared the lady's disappointment, since he loved to see people wearing Christmas jumpers; and although he hadn't noticed many this year, he had spotted a large winking robin on one festive sweater. Rejoice had winked at the woman wearing it and he was sure she had winked back at him.

'She must like robins,' thought Rejoice, 'but then, everyone seems to like robins at this time of year.'

December is the season of the robin. During the last few weeks, Rejoice had seen himself everywhere – on cards and candles, cups and calendars, even on slippers and socks!

The loud lady continued her conversation and Rejoice continued to listen. He gathered that she had left her Christmas shopping a bit late and now, all in a panic, she had to hurry to the High Street to make some last-minute purchases.

'But she had better be quick,' thought the robin, 'because the shops will be closing early today.'

The lady left the bench, still talking loudly into her phone, but Rejoice remained where he was, musing and reminiscing. He thought about his own visits to the shops in central London, where sometimes, very early in the morning, he would perch on posts and traffic lights and look into shop windows.

A few years ago, not long after dawn, the little bird had flown from Hyde Park to Harrods to see its famous Christmas windows. One display had particularly caught his eye because it reminded him of a trip he once took to Scandinavia, which he liked a lot. Rejoice had sat

on railings outside the shop for some time, gazing into the Land of Make-Believe – a winter window world of Scandinavian snow, silver birch trees and Santa's sleigh, out of which had fallen lots of toys, including a robin who sat on the head of a large bear, staring out of the window.

Rejoice had returned to the massive department store later in the day, and from a distance he had watched people passing by. Many turned to look at its displays, but just as many turned away.

'I wonder why they weren't interested,' thought the robin. 'Perhaps they had places to go and people to see, things to do and places to be . . . things to do and places to be . . . things to do and places to be. . . .'

Rejoice suddenly sat up straight, and with some alarm he remembered that he had things to do and places to be. He had been sitting on his bench in Regent's Park for a long time – a very long time – and he was surprised to find that, like the visitors, daylight had drained away from the green jewel and the park was now closed. It was getting cold and the robin felt unsettled. He was annoyed with himself that he had become distracted and had spent so long thinking about phones and clothes and shops and

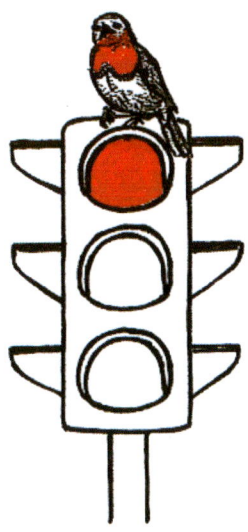

toys that he hadn't given a thought to his Christmas Day carol for some time. It would be midnight in a few hours and he still hadn't decided which carol to sing.

Rejoice began to feel a little sad. He pictured the Land of Make-Believe and, with a heavy heart, he remembered that the lavish windows full of fantastic gifts really were only make-believe for many people. The displays were just a dream for the folk who would be too poor to eat tonight.

'No wonder so many of them didn't want to look,' thought the robin, and his spirits sank further when he thought of the homeless pavement people who would not be enjoying the bright lights of London this Christmas, but instead would be sheltering in the shadows on the city's streets. 'How many people will be lonely?' lamented the tiny bird. 'How many will be hungry and hurting? How many will receive no gifts and have no gifts to give?'

And then, from deep within his heart, Rejoice heard a quiet call:

Give your love! Give your love!

It sounded like the soft voice of a dove, but Rejoice had heard it before and he recognised that it was no earthly voice.

The quiet call came again:

Give your love! Give your love!

The robin knew there was only one way he could answer the call, and that was with a song. So he began to sing. His carol cut the cold, clear evening air as it rang across the park in piercing purity:

In the bleak midwinter, frosty wind made moan,
Earth stood hard as iron, water like a stone;
Snow had fallen snow on snow, snow on snow,
In the bleak midwinter, long ago.

Our God, Heaven cannot hold Him, nor earth sustain,
Heaven and earth shall flee away when He comes to reign.
In the bleak midwinter a stable-place sufficed
The Lord God Almighty, Jesus Christ.

Enough for Him, whom cherubim worship night and day,
A breastful of milk and a mangerful of hay,
Enough for Him whom angels fall down before,
The ox and ass and camel which adore.

What can I give Him, poor as I am?
If I were a shepherd I would bring a lamb,
If I were a wise man I would do my part,
Yet what I can I give Him, give my heart.

Had Rejoice found his Christmas Day carol? It was a song that had to be sung because, if people really listened to its message and gave their heart, gave their love, the world would, without doubt, be a better place.

It was now dark. In a few hours the robin would return to Big Ben, but there was one last place in the park he wanted to visit before the day was over, and that place was Primrose Hill.

Rejoice left one bench and flew off across Regent's Park to sit on another. The bird's new bench was a perch with a view, and what a view it was! Rejoice had always loved looking at London from the hill – especially at night, when the town twinkled in the dark like a brilliant diamond. It was certainly a city full of treasures, and the robin felt a surge of excitement at the sight of the mighty metropolis stretching out before him as far as the eye could see, heaving with history.

'So much to sit on and sing about,' thought Rejoice.

He felt blessed that he was a bird – a creature with the gift of song and flight, free to fly above the land and enjoy a bird's-eye view of life. His wide, far-reaching perspective gave him wisdom, and tonight, as he gazed across central London towards the place where he began the day, Rejoice asked his wisdom to help him make an important decision.

'Which carol does the world need to hear tomorrow?' Rejoice pondered and reflected.

He thought back to the places he had been and the people he had seen, the things he had done and the history he had sung. Who had moved him most this year? The robin felt he had learned something from all the anniversaries he had celebrated, but there was one in particular that he couldn't forget because it was all about remembrance. It was an anniversary story that seemed to sum up all the sacrifice, courage and loyalty he had sung about. Rejoice thought back to Armistice Sunday. He recalled how, at eleven o'clock on the eleventh day of the eleventh month, the Spirit of Peace had moved across the land, uniting people of every colour, character and condition in His healing presence as they remembered those who had died in war. That same Spirit had visited the weary world one hundred years ago in 1918,

during the Armistice that ended the Great War. But there was also an earlier armistice moment in the war which Rejoice and many others had heard of – a ceasefire that occurred at the beginning of World War One, which his ancestors had often sung about, and it was this armistice that Rejoice wanted to remember again tonight.

On Christmas Eve in 1914, a ray of hope lit the Western Front when a carol carried across the desolation and darkness of no-man's-land. It had been sung by soldiers in a section of the German trench and had been answered by a song from soldiers in the British trench. The initial musical exchange had led to more carol-singing and had created a moment of merriment amidst the mayhem of war, during which hostilities were halted for a brief time, and men were blessed by the Spirit of Peace and Goodwill . . . the Spirit of Christmas . . . the Spirit of Love.

A cascade of crystal-clear notes suddenly fell from the robin's bill like drops of water from a fountain. He bounced along the top of the bench and then flew up into the sky above Primrose Hill, dancing in the air with delight. His heart blazed with realisation as the words of his Christmas Day carol shone before him. It had been sung by soldiers

on Christmas Eve in 1914 and Rejoice knew that the world needed to hear it tonight. It was time to turn to the Light and find the peace that only Love can give . . .

>Silent night, holy night!
>All is calm, all is bright,
>Round yon virgin mother and child,
>Holy Infant so tender and mild,
>Sleep in heavenly peace,
>Sleep in heavenly peace.
>
>Silent night, holy night!
>Shepherds quake at the sight,
>Glories stream from heaven afar,
>Heavenly hosts sing "Alleluia!"
>Christ the Saviour is born!
>Christ the Saviour is born!
>
>Silent night, holy night!
>Son of God, love's pure light!
>Radiance beams from Thy holy face
>With the dawn of redeeming grace,
>Jesus, Lord at Thy birth!
>Jesus, Lord at Thy birth!

Rejoice had found his Christmas Day carol! His heart burned with joy – a joy that warmed the flame on his red breast, a joy that, at midnight, would kindle his Flamesong. He knew that tonight robins all over the world would sing their own Flamesong and their message would be understood by all who heard it because, tonight, they would sing a song of Love.

It was now very late. Rejoice left his bench and flew down to an oak on the side of Primrose Hill known as Shakespeare's Tree. It had been planted many moons ago to mark the anniversary of the bard's birth. The robin frequently perched in it. He sat on a branch near the top of the oak and his tiny body sparkled against a star-studded sky like a bright bauble in a Christmas tree.

Rejoice was tired and needed to rest before returning to Big Ben, but before he settled himself to sleep he decided to sing one last song. The robin puffed out his chest and took a deep breath of cold, crisp air. Then he opened his beautiful bill. . . .

People often spoke of the old oak and the day they heard it sing.

I heard a robin on Primrose Hill,
His voice was golden and brown was his bill,
And he sang for joy, sang for joy,
He sang for joy in the sunshine.

I heard a robin in Regent's Park,
His red breast blazed in a flaming heart,
And he sang for joy, sang for joy,
He sang for joy in the sunshine.